DRAGON TALES

This is the first of the Dragon Tales Chronicles.
Coming soon:
Dragon Tales Book Two: Quest for a Friend
Dragon Tales Book Three: Quest for Adventure

DRAGON TALES

BOOK ONE

Quest for a Cave

by

Judy Hayman

illustrated by

Caroline Wolfe Murray

First published in Great Britain by Practical
Inspiration Publishing, 2014

ISBN (print): 978-1-910056-08-0
ISBN (ebook): 978-1-910056-09-7

For Phoebe, who was in at the beginning.
And in memory of my mother.

Table of contents

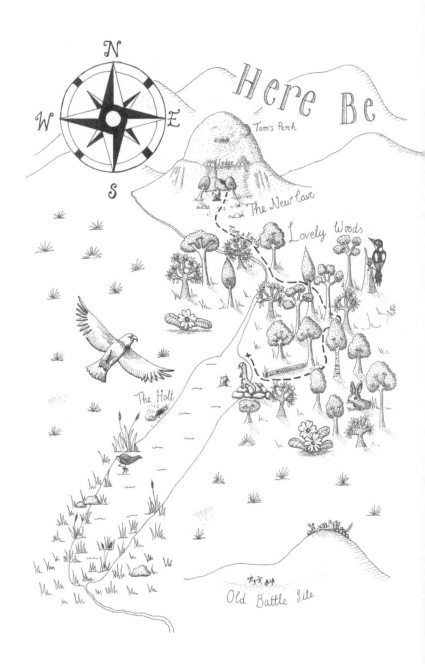

Chapter 1

Trouble with Tails

Emily was feeling grumpy, which was not like her at all. She usually enjoyed reading in bed without her young brother Tom pestering her, but today the story was irritating her.

Why did children in books have such exciting adventures? They were *Humans*—they couldn't even fly! She was a DRAGON, with wings and scales and a spiky tail. She might be small, but she could breathe fire—though not very well yet. She lived in a cave! Life should be far more dangerous and adventurous for her.

But it wasn't.

The cave where she lived with her family was at the head of a quiet glen in the Highlands of Scotland. It was well hidden by boulders and gorse bushes. Mum

and Dad liked it because it was safe and no Humans had ever been seen there. Emily knew it was unlikely that a knight in shining armour would ever be seen in the glen, but even a stray hiker in a woolly hat would be better than nothing.

She wanted to see one of these famous Humans that her father was so anxious to keep away from. She wanted to see the world beyond their glen. She wanted some other dragons living near enough to have adventures with; obviously not huge black Bulgarian dragons or fierce spiky Chinese Reds, but some other Scottish Blues like her own family, or little Welsh Greens like her grandparents.

She felt like throwing her book into a far corner of the cave, but she hadn't quite finished the story and was afraid it would get charred by mistake so she tucked it under her heather pillow.

She was about to get up when her father called, "Up you get Emily! Will you fetch Tom back for breakfast?" He was stirring porridge in a pot on the fire. Emily crawled out of bed and shook herself to get rid of the bits.

"Be careful," said Dad, "you nearly got bits in the porridge!"

"It might make it taste better," said Emily, and skipped out of the way as Dad sent a small huff of flame after her for being cheeky.

At the door of the cave she stopped and looked for Tom. He was a little way up the hill, crouching down with his back to her. Instead of shouting, as she usually did, she crept up the hill quietly to see what he was doing.

Tom was lying on his front on a stony patch. He had built a little pile of twigs and dry grass and was breathing heavily. Emily knew what he was doing. He was trying to Huff. Young dragons can't Huff properly. They can breathe out a puff of smoke almost as soon as they hatch from their Egg, but real fire comes later. All winter Tom had been grumpy, because Emily, who was three years older, could breathe out *real* flames. She couldn't manage to light the cooking fire yet, but she was working on it.

"BOO!!" she said. Tom jumped, and then pretended he had heard her coming. But she knew he hadn't.

"It's no good, Tom," she said. "You'll just have to wait 'til you're old enough. Dad says the porridge is ready."

"I don't want any," said Tom grumpily.

"Yes you do! You're always hungry." She gave him a shove to get him up. He shoved back. So to show him who was in charge, she gave a little huff in the direction of his pile of twigs. Her flames were just strong enough, and the little fire blazed merrily.

"Easy peasy!" she said.

Tom scowled. "I was nearly there!" he shouted. "Now you've spoiled it! You always do!" Crossly he swung his long blue tail sideways and knocked Emily off her feet. Then he flew out of her way and glided down the mountain to the cave. When he landed, he looked up at Emily, who was still sprawling by his little fire.

"The porridge is getting cold!" he yelled, and disappeared into the cave.

Emily got to her four feet slowly. She felt bruised and cross. "Little brothers are such pests," she thought. "I wish I had a sister. Or a friend. This glen is so boring! I need to find a friend to have adventures with!"

She shook her wings and carefully jumped the fire out as her Dad had taught her at her first Huff. ("Never leave a fire, even a little one," he had said, "you don't know where it might end up!")

"Where's Mum?" she asked as she limped back to the cave. One leg was sore and her right wing felt a bit crumpled.

"Collecting firewood. She should be back any minute," said Dad, ladling her porridge.

At that moment, both Tom and Emily spotted three distinct puffs of white smoke rising above the trees opposite.

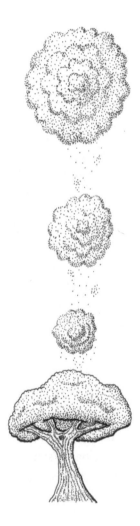

"Three puffs!" shouted Emily. "She wants some help."

"I'll go!" said Tom, shovelling in the last of his porridge.

"No, I will. There must be too much wood for her to manage by herself," said Dad. "You can't carry a big load. I won't be long."

He spread his big wings and soared down the valley towards the smoke.

Tom scowled. "I bet I could."

"No you couldn't," said Emily. "You're not strong enough."

"Stronger than you!"

"Not!"

"AM!!"

Soon there were two spiky tails duelling furiously. It was quite an even duel, even though she was bigger, because Tom lashed his tail more wildly. They only stopped when they saw both their parents flying slowly towards them, each carrying a big load of pine branches for the fire.

"Quarrelling again!" said Mum when she had landed and got her breath back. "Where's my porridge? I'm hungry enough for two helpings."

They finished their breakfast with mugs of hot nettle tea and when he was full Tom was cheerful again, and Emily felt less grumpy. Mum smoothed out her wing with a few gentle huffs.

"No more fighting!" she said. "Go inside and tidy your beds while I wash the bowls."

She flew down to the stream, while Dad made a start on breaking up the branches into sticks for the fire. He carried the first pile into the cave and stacked it at the back next to the stores of food. There wasn't much room by the time the second pile was in. Emily and Tom tried to tidy their heather beds, but every time they were neat *someone's* tail messed them up again. When Mum came back and saw the state of the cave, she sighed.

"Everybody outside," she said, "Too many tails in here!"

"Wings are useful, but tails are more trouble than they're worth," Emily declared as she followed her Dad outside.

"I like mine," said Tom. "It's got a good swish." He was jumping the last of the sticks into small pieces.

"It's very useful when you've got an itch between your wings," said Dad. "I wouldn't want to be without mine!"

"I suppose so," said Emily. "But they do take up a lot of room, and Tom never stops twitching his, even when he's asleep."

Mum came out. "I know what the trouble is," she said. "It isn't just tails, it's this cave. It's too small for a growing family. I think we should move cave."

"Brilliant!" Tom shouted. "Let's look for one near a loch for swimming!"

"I want one near another dragon family with some girls of my age."

"No, boys!"

"Just somewhere bigger, with space to get away from young dragons when they're arguing!" said Mum wearily.

"Hold on, hold on!" said Dad loudly. "It sounds a nice idea, but new caves aren't easy to find. Not empty ones. The good thing about this place is that it's

NEVER visited by prying Humans. If we move we'll be spotted for sure. And you all know what *that* will lead to! Knights on quests, kids with cameras, hunters with guns even! No, better safe than sorry. We'll stay put."

He flew off for a drink of stream water before anyone could argue, leaving his family to heave three heavy sighs; a big flame, a little flame and a small puff of grey smoke.

"I wonder how we change his mind?" said Mum softly to herself.

Chapter 2

Expeditions

A ll through that day, Emily dreamed of a new cave. In her imagination, there were two caves in a mountainside, and in the one next door there was a friend who wanted adventures too!

In the afternoon, the four of them flew up the mountain on a foraging expedition, to collect beetles for broth. While Emily searched, she wondered what it would be like to live somewhere else. She had spent all her life on this hillside.

"It shouldn't be *that* difficult to find a new cave," she muttered to herself.

"Don't you believe it!" said Dad, coming up behind her and making her jump; she hadn't realised that she had said it out loud. "Where would you start looking?"

"In the book I'm reading," Emily began, "there are four children—young Humans, I mean. They *always* find a cave when they need one, wherever they are— mountains or islands or valleys. And every cave is big enough to live in and no-one ever finds them. There's always a spring of fresh water nearby too," she added. "So I don't see why we can't *look*, at least. We're *bound* to find one."

"Huh, books!" said her father. "You can never believe what you read in *books*. In books, glens like this would be full of men on horseback, with big swords and feathers in their hats. I've never even seen a *horse* up here, have you?"

"There're some little hairy ones down by the loch," said Tom swooping nearer and then flying off without waiting to hear what the conversation was about.

"Can you see a knight on one of those?" his father scoffed. "Forget it, Emily. Books are just books; you can't believe a word they say." He flew up to join Tom, who was practising flying upside down.

Emily sighed. Her mum came up and put a wing around her. "Nothing wrong with books," she whispered. "You keep reading and finding ideas. I have a feeling we're going to need them soon!"

They flew home for supper carrying their beetles. It was good broth!

That night Emily finished her book, which featured a particularly fine cave which the four children had to leave behind when they were rescued by something called an 'aeroplane'. She had started by envying those children, having adventures all together, but now she pitied them. Fancy having no wings of your own! She snuggled into her heather. "Mum's on my side," she thought as she fell asleep. "She wants a new cave too."

The next morning was misty and Dad announced that he was going fishing in the loch lower down the glen.

"Can I come?" Emily and Tom shouted together.

"No," said Dad. "You need peace and quiet for fishing."

"Yes!" said Mum very firmly. "If we're to carry on living in this wretched little cave, it needs careful rearranging, and I can't do that with you three in the way. You can take them both out for the day."

Dad opened his mouth to argue, looked at Mum and changed his mind.

Mum packed them a picnic, gave Dad the bag and shooed them off down the glen.

It felt mysterious flying down the glen through the mist. Emily liked it. She couldn't see the ground, but they weren't flying very high because they could clearly hear the stream hurrying down the glen to the loch. It was quite a bit bigger—almost a river—by the time it reached the bottom of the glen. Dad led them down to a flat grassy bank near the place where the stream tumbled over rocks into the calm waters of the loch. They glided down and landed, scaring a heron which flapped off crossly as they arrived.

"Right!" said Dad, putting down the picnic bag. "There are three ways to catch fish. You can fish like that heron—stand still in the shallow water, then make a grab when one comes near. That's quite easy, but the fish are small at the edge. If you want a big fish, you have to dive into the deep water like an osprey and come up with one in your talons. This needs practice, and you are NOT to try it! The third way is the easiest of all, but that can wait until after lunch. I think the mist is clearing down here. You two find places to stand at the edge—not too close to each other—and I'll do some diving. Good luck!"

He flew over the loch and they watched him fly slowly up and down close to the water, looking down intently. Suddenly he dived! There was a flurry of water and up he came with a trout in his talons. He soared back to them and dropped the fish beside their bag. Emily and Tom cheered loudly, but Dad hushed them.

"You have to be *quiet* to catch fish," he said, and flew back to the middle of the loch.

"I think I'll stand where that heron was," said Emily. "I expect it knows all the best places."

"Huh, what does an old bird know?" Tom scoffed. "I'll go over there. I bet I catch more than you."

He moved along the bank, and then waded a little way into the water. Emily saw him peer down so closely that the end of his nose was almost touching the surface. She smiled. He was taking this fishing very seriously. She saw him pounce and miss. She wasn't very keen on putting her head in the water, so she decided to use a talon instead. The water felt very cold around her claws, but she soon got used to it, and in a few minutes had caught her first little fish. She wondered if Human children could catch fish. Perhaps today she might actually see one! She looked around hopefully, but the only moving things were her father, far out over the water, and a few worried rabbits nibbling the grass with their ears twitching. There was another fish. Snatch! That was two!

By lunchtime, the sun had come out, and Dad had caught five fine trout and laid them in a row on the grass. Emily and Tom had four each. Emily was pleased that they were even. She was quite enjoying this peaceful day, and didn't feel like quarrelling.

They opened the picnic bag and found chunks of cold spicy rabbit, charcoal crunchies and a bottle of nettle fizz. As a special treat, Mum had packed a little bag of stripy Bumblebugs, which they all crunched happily. Obviously she wasn't as cross as she had sounded!

"Now for a spot of lazy fishing," Dad said with his mouth full. He lay on his back on the bank and dangled his tail, with its pointed end, into the water. "If you keep it twitching very slightly, the fish get themselves hooked," he said. "Try it and see." He shut his eyes.

Emily and Tom looked at each other.

"Dad, can we explore a bit instead? We won't get lost," pleaded Emily. "We'll be back by the time you wake—I mean—finish fishing."

"All right," said Dad, "but no flying. Keep yourselves out of sight. You can't be too careful on a sunny day." He settled back happily and closed his eyes.

Chapter 3

Yellow Dragons

Emily and Tom crept towards the bracken at the edge of the loch, sucking Bumblebugs. "Which way?" asked Tom. "Up or down?"

"Down!" said Emily firmly. "Creep along the edge of the loch and let's see what's at the other end where the stream runs out."

As quietly as they could they wriggled their way through the bracken, skirting outcrops of grey rock that sparkled with quartz in the sun. The heron flew over them, peering down suspiciously. There were so many insects in the air that it felt as if they were crawling through Mum's broth. Tom longed to swish them away, but he knew Emily would frown round at him if he made any noise. (Fortunately a dragon's hide is too thick for most insects, though a full grown and determined Scottish Midge can get through even an adult dragon if it's really hungry.)

Suddenly there was a loud rustle in the bracken, the fronds parted and one of the little hairy horses lifted its head and stared at them in surprise. It shook its head and snorted loudly. Tom snorted back. The pony was so surprised by the puff of smoke that it reared up, turned on its heels and pounded off. They heard the noise of several sets of hooves, and when they peered cautiously above the heather they saw four ponies cantering away, long manes and tails flying.

"Huh, they wouldn't be much use to a knight. Dead easy to scare!" said Tom happily. "We're nearly at the end of the loch. Let's have a look."

"Careful then," said Emily. She knew that it was risky to venture into the open, but she was longing to see what was round the corner.

At this end of the little loch, two hills almost met, and the river fell over a tumble of rocks in the gap and disappeared over the edge. The two little dragons had no idea what was beyond—they had never ventured as far as this before. They clambered carefully over the rocks, balanced on two big ones and looked down. Then they gasped in surprise.

The river fell in a series of short waterfalls to a second, bigger loch about half a mile away. This one even had islands, and the biggest of the islands had trees growing on it. Emily recognised it immediately as the sort of place where the children in her books might have adventures, but there were no Humans to be seen anywhere. It was wild and lonely and perfect for dragons. And to their surprise, THERE WERE DRAGONS THERE!

In the distance, on the loch bank where the valley widened out, three large dragons were standing quite still. Two were looking down at the water, but one had its head in the air and seemed to be staring right at them. They were bright yellow. They looked quite small, but Emily and Tom knew that they were a long way away, and would be enormous close up. All around them the grass and heather had been torn and trampled into a muddy mess.

"There must have been a battle," said Emily, "and these dragons won, and now they're sleeping, except that one that's looking at us. Quick, get back to Dad before it flies up here and attacks us!"

Slipping and sliding, they made their way as fast as they could back to their path, where they crouched to get their breath back and listened. There was no sound of flapping wings. There was a haze over the sun now, and they knew the mist would be coming back when the evening came on. They hurried as fast as they could and soon came to the place where they had left their father. He was still asleep! Emily couldn't believe it. She felt as if they had been away for hours.

Tom hurried ahead and took a flying leap onto his father's tummy. "Dad, wake up!" he panted. "Dragons, yellow dragons . . ."

"Wha-a-a-t? Get off, Tom! What are you talking about?" Dad rolled over and got up, shaking drops of water off his tail.

"It's true, Dad! We crept to the end of the loch and looked down and there are three huge yellow dragons sitting by the water down the valley," said Emily in a rush.

"*Yellow* dragons?"

"Yes!"

"Did they see you?"

"I don't know. They didn't fly up. But we came away as fast as we could."

"I'd better go and see. You two stay here." Dad said. "And don't move!" he added as he spread his wings and flew low over the loch. They watched anxiously, and saw him land a little way from the rocks, then crawl cautiously into the gap in the hills and peer over.

"He shows up against the sky, because he's such a dark blue!" Emily worried, trying to keep her teeth from chattering. She noticed that Tom had crept close to her side and was very quiet. What if Dad was attacked? She would have to get Tom home safely. Would he be strong enough to fly home? Dad usually gave him a lift. What if . . .

A sudden loud roar in the distance echoed round the hills. The two little dragons wrapped their wings round their ears and crouched together, trembling. In a few minutes they heard the flap of wings, and Emily risked a look up. Dad landed beside them.

"Quick, pack up! We need to get home." He bundled the fish into the empty picnic bag. "Right, on my back both of you. I'll fly low, so hold tight if I have to swerve around the trees. We need to keep out of sight. Emily, you on the back, Tom in front. Hold the bag tight. We don't want to lose the fish. Ready?"

It was a breathless scramble, but very soon Dad was airborne, weaving through the trees until he reached the higher slopes where the bushes were lower and he could fly faster. Emily looked back, but couldn't see anything following them.

"I think we're all right," she said. "Do you want me to fly myself now?"

"No," panted her father. "I can manage. Nearly there."

"Did those dragons see you, Dad?" asked Tom, who was rapidly recovering from his fright. "Will we have to fight them? I bet I'd win!"

"They're not dragons," said Dad, grimly, as their cave came into sight and they saw Mum carrying a bundle of new heather in through the doorway. "It's much worse than that!"

Chapter 4

Midnight Adventure

D ad refused to talk about their day until the supper had been cooked and eaten. Despite feeling just a bit sick after the swerving flight up the mountain, Emily enjoyed her barbecued trout. She and Tom ate their own little fish—three each. (Emily suspected that the heron had pinched two while her father was asleep, but she didn't say anything.) Their parents shared the big ones, crunching the bones hungrily. Afterwards Mum made hot drinks and they sat in the cave entrance as the stars came out and darkness fell over the valley.

"Now," said Dad quietly, "No roaring or huffing tonight. We need to be quiet. This is serious. Those yellow things you thought were dragons were *really* creatures belonging to Humans. I even saw a Human climb onto one. I heard it roar at him!"

He described to Mum all that he had seen from the edge of the loch. She was horrified to think that Emily and Tom had been allowed to go exploring by themselves, but decided not to start an argument about it.

"Will they bother us?" she asked. "They're a long way away. Can they fly?"

"I don't think so," said Dad. "They had long necks and very strange feet, but I couldn't see any wings. When one of them roared, I saw it tearing up the ground by the loch, so it must have been looking for food for the Human. But I'm worried. We've never had Humans so close to us before, and we know they bring trouble. We need to find out more about these yellow monsters, and the sooner the better. It's dark tonight, so I'm going to fly down there and see what's going on. I'll take Emily. You stay here with Tom."

Emily was so surprised that she choked on her last mouthful of nettle tea and couldn't speak at all for several minutes. But Tom and Mum had plenty to say!

"THAT'S NOT FAIR!"

"I won't have you taking Emily into danger, Duncan! It's bad enough that you let them wander off this afternoon. Anything might happen . . . It's their bedtime. NO!"

"WHY CAN'T I GO TOO?"

"SSSHH!!" said Dad. "I said no shouting and huffing! I might need Emily, Gwen, and she'll be quite safe with me. I can fly her back if I need to. We'll go now, and we won't be long. We have to find out what's happening down there. Come on Emily."

Tom was furious and stomped off into the cave to sulk.

With a final cough and splutter, Emily got to her feet. She was so excited she hardly heard Mum's worried instructions about the dangers of flying in the dark. Dad spread his wings and looked down at her.

"Keep close beside me," he said. "If we glide, we'll make very little noise, and if we fly high we'll miss the trees. Ready?"

Emily nodded. "Bye, Mum," she said. "Don't worry, I'll be fine." She spread her wings and took off as soon as her father said "GO!"

The two dragons rose higher and higher until Mum and the cooking fire seemed very small beneath them. Then they set a course for the first loch. Dragons can see quite well in the dark, and Emily spotted several deer grazing by the stream as they flew over. A stag with spreading antlers looked up at them suspiciously but didn't roar a challenge. She saw owls hunting nearer the ground, but they were looking down and didn't spot the dragons gliding above them.

When they reached the far end of the loch, Dad pointed silently at the rocks, and they both landed carefully. Emily was pleased with herself. It had been a long fast flight and she had kept up with Dad and wasn't even out of breath. They both peered down towards the place where the yellow dragons had stood. They were still there, looking like strange grey shapes in the starlight. The dragons crouched, staring for several minutes, but nothing moved down the valley and the only sound was of water and wind.

"I think it's safe," Dad whispered in Emily's ear. "We'll go down. Follow me."

This time they didn't fly high, because Dad knew that they might show up even in the night sky. Instead they kept low, with the hill behind them, so they were almost invisible as they took short flights and the odd scramble down beside the stream to the second loch. When they reached it, they tiptoed to a line of low gorse bushes and found a rough path leading in the right direction. Emily followed Dad, careful to keep her wings tucked in tight so that they wouldn't get hooked up on the prickly gorse. She could feel her heart beating fast.

Suddenly Dad stopped and Emily almost fell over the end of his tail. The thick gorse came to an end with broken branches lying all over the ground, and blocking their way was a high fence made of thick wire netting. Emily had never seen anything like it before, but she didn't think it would be a problem to them.

"Shall we fly over?" she whispered.

"Not yet," her father replied. "Let's follow it round and see where it goes."

They turned away from the loch and crept round the outside of the fence as it marched towards the line of trees at the foot of the hill. When it turned the corner they did too, until Emily felt as though they had been creeping along for hours. There didn't seem to be anything interesting on the other side of the fence not even the usual night-time animals. The sky was getting lighter, and she realised that the moon was rising behind the hill. What would happen if the yellow dragons spotted them in the moonlight?

The fence turned another corner and they saw an extraordinary sight. A wide gap had been cut in the trees and bushes and a churned-up muddy track led away from the fence and disappeared down the valley. They saw fallen trees and piles of earth and stones and strange shaped hummocks beside the road. As they turned to look through to the other side of the fence, Emily gasped in horror.

One of the strange yellow dragons was squatting quite near to them; it loomed above her, huge, still and silent with its nose on the ground.

Chapter 5

Danger—Humans!

Close up, it didn't look as much like a dragon as she had thought when she had seen it in the distance. It had no wings that she could see, and its legs were most peculiar—round and black. Even more strange, there were letters written on it—"J.C.B." Whoever heard of a creature with a label on, she thought. In the brightening moonlight she could see the others further away, all looking the same and all asleep.

Her father touched her wing. "I'm going over," he whispered. "I don't think there's anything alive in there, but I need to make sure. Stay here and don't move. If you hear me roar, get away up the mountain and back to Mum as fast as you can. All right?"

"Yes," said Emily, trying to sound brave.

"Good girl!" He gave her a tiny huff then, with a flying leap, was over the fence and beside the yellow dragon. He touched it with one claw, and Emily heard a tiny metallic *ting*. She waited for the dragon to wake up, but it didn't move. Dad came back to the fence.

"I thought so," he whispered through the wire, "they're not alive at all. This is some sort of machine. There's Human mischief going on here. I'm going further in." He disappeared behind the machine and Emily was left alone. She shivered. The strange machine seemed to loom larger and larger on the other side of the fence. She wanted to call out to Dad. She wanted to be back in the cave with Mum and Tom. She wished...

Suddenly Dad was back. "You need to come over," he whispered. "It's quite safe at the moment, but there's something I want to show you."

Emily took a few steps away from the fence, then made a flying leap, cleared the wire, and landed beside Dad. "Well done," he said, patting her head. "Come over here."

Emily followed him across the churned-up mud, glancing nervously around. There didn't seem to be anything moving, but it was spooky all the same. The moon came up over the hill and lit up muddy puddles and the wire and the yellow machines, and in front of them was a squat building with steps leading up to a door. It wasn't very big, but Emily shuddered. She wasn't used to square buildings—or doors. They weren't natural, like caves. Dad stopped beside a big flat square set upright on two posts.

"This is why I brought you," he whispered. "I thought we might find something like this. I think the answer to the mystery is in the letters written here. Can you read them?"

Emily peered in the moonlight and slowly read aloud;

Laggan Loch Outdoor Centre

Water Sports, Climbing, Pony Trekking.
Self Catering Chalets   Bar and Restaurant
Building Contractors: McTaggert and Co.

"I knew it!" Dad exclaimed. "Well done, Emily. I always said all that reading of yours would come in useful!"

"But what does it mean?"

"It means that this glen will soon be swarming with Humans. They're going to put square buildings everywhere. That's what these machines are for. They'll cut down the trees, ruin the peace and quiet and drive away the animals. It will kill the whole glen!" She had never seen Dad so angry. He sent a furious spurt of flame into the night sky.

Suddenly they were blinded by a brilliant white light. Emily screamed and hid her eyes with her wings. She felt Dad press close to protect her. Then the door of the hut burst open, and a real live Human stood in the doorway. Peering in terror, she heard a voice cry, "WHAT THE ... !!" and saw the man start down the steps towards them.

"FLY!" yelled Dad, giving her a push. She obeyed, but when she was above the fence she turned and looked back. She saw the man reach her father and screamed again. Then Dad swung his long spiked tail

and knocked the man to the ground, where he lay still, face down in the mud. She hovered while Dad flipped the man onto his back, and then flew up to join her.

"Back up the hillside," he said breathlessly. They landed by a big rock, and peered round it at the enclosure with its machines and its hut, still weirdly lit up in the night. Nothing moved.

"Did you kill him, Dad?"

"No, but he won't wake up for a while! It looks as though he's the only one, but I wanted to be sure."

With a startling suddenness the light went out. The night seemed much blacker and full of dangers.

Dad took a deep breath and put a wing round Emily. "Come on, let's get home. Your mother will be worrying. Are you tired?"

"No."

"We'll fly home high and straight. Follow me."

They took off and headed back up the hill. Emily tried her best to keep up, but her wings kept drooping and she flew slower and lower. Eventually Dad realised and came back for her. She climbed onto his back and they flew on, faster now, until their own hillside appeared below them. Mum was still outside the cave, watching out for them. She waved as Dad circled and came to land beside the dying fire. Emily tumbled off his back.

"Mum, you'll never guess . . ." she began, but Dad interrupted.

"No more tonight," he said. "We'll talk about this in the morning. It's very late. Bed!"

"Try not to wake Tom," Mum said. "I'll come and tuck you up in a minute."

But when she went quietly into the cave a few minutes later, she found that Emily was already fast asleep, tired out after an adventure just as exciting as the ones in her favourite books.

Chapter 6

Start of the Search

Emily woke very late next morning. Tom had been hauled out of bed and taken outside as soon as he was awake, so that he wouldn't disturb her. He was so keen to hear about the strange dragons that he had forgotten his sulks of the night before, and was trying to talk Dad into a raid on their lair. "We could burn the place up, Dad! Can you eat Humans? Cooked first, obviously..." he was saying through mouthfuls of porridge as she came out, yawning.

Mum cuffed him with a wing. "Tom, that's revolting! Calm down and finish your breakfast. Here's yours, Emily."

While Emily ate her breakfast, they gathered together to decide what to do.

"There's no time to waste," said Dad. "If that man wakes up and says he saw dragons they'll be out looking for us. Even if he doesn't, we know that this glen will soon be over-run with Humans so we can't stay here."

"I have *just* spring-cleaned this cave!" Mum exclaimed. "You said we had to stay. Make up your mind!"

"That was yesterday," said Dad. "Today is different. There's no time to lose. We'll go cave-hunting right away."

Tom spread his wings. "Let's go!" he said excitedly.

"Hold on," said Mum. "This needs planning."

"We have to go NOW!" Tom danced up and down impatiently until he took off by mistake and had to be hauled back down by the tail.

"Sit down, Tom," said Dad. "Mum's right. There's no point in flying round in circles. We have to decide which way to go."

"Have you any ideas?" asked Mum. "You've flown further afield than I have."

"Well," said Dad thoughtfully, "we know that *down* the glen is no use, and I don't think higher up

39

the mountains would be very comfortable in winter. But if you fly over that ridge to the south west you come to a stretch of empty moorland which is no use to us because there's nowhere to hide. But I did fly over it years ago, and eventually you come to an unusual mountain outcrop. It's steep and knobbly on the way up but with a round smooth summit which makes it easy to find. It might be a good place for caves. Shall we try there?"

"Yes!" said Tom enthusiastically.

"We can always come back and try in a different direction if the knobbly hill is no good," said Emily. This was the most exciting thing that had happened in ages! "Can we start right now?"

"We must hide everything in the cave. Leave no traces outside in case any Humans come looking while we're away."

"We'll take the food," Mum said. "If it's a day's flying, we'll have to camp somewhere for the night. Tom, come and help."

They prepared for the journey as fast as they could, but it was late morning by the time they were ready. Emily kept glancing down the glen, expecting to see a horde of fierce Humans searching for them, but nobody came.

As they set off it began to rain, a gentle steady drizzle, but dragons have good thick hide, and as Dad said, the worst thing on a long flight is a strong wind, not rain. It meant that they couldn't see very far ahead which was a pity, Emily thought, but it would keep them safer. And the moor was not very interesting— just endless bracken and heather and peaty pools and patches of bright green which Emily knew hid dangerous marshy ground. In the drizzle it looked flat and empty. As she flew, she thought of the knobbly hill and hoped with all her might that there would be other dragons living there.

They flew on and on. Both young dragons had a rest now and then, riding on their parents' backs. After two hours' steady flight, they came down to land on a stony patch beside two huge boulders, and sheltered between them while they ate a late picnic lunch.

After their rest, they flew a little faster and the landscape beneath them began to change into hummocky hills with small lochs and streams. They saw a few herds of deer below and a pair of suspicious eagles flew above them for a while, keeping a close eye on the dragons from a safe distance before sheering away and disappearing from sight. It was getting towards dusk, and Emily was beginning to think that Dad was completely lost, when he suddenly pointed and in the distance she could see the vague shape of a very odd-looking mountain.

"That's it," he said. "We can't get there before dark. We'll camp tonight, and first thing tomorrow morning, we'll go on a proper cave-hunt."

"There's a place down there in amongst those pine trees," Mum said, and led them on a gentle glide to land.

Emily and Tom were almost too tired to keep their eyes open, so Mum quickly gathered some bracken for beds while Dad cooked supper with Huff to save trying to light a fire with damp wood. As soon as they had eaten, Tom and Emily rolled into their bracken and fell asleep, and very soon after their parents joined them, curling round to keep them warm.

"I hope we find somewhere drier tomorrow," Mum murmured as they settled down. "This damp is getting through my hide!

"It might stop raining," Dad said hopefully, but the only reply was a sleepy snort.

Chapter 7

The Mysterious Mountain

Next morning the dragons woke early and shivered in their damp beds, even though the rain had stopped and a watery sun was peering through the trees.

"Let's risk a fire," said Mum, and she and Dad huffed their hardest until finally the damp wood caught. They spread their wings and gradually felt drier and warmer and more ready to face a day's exploring.

"Right," said Dad, when they had packed the few scraps of food that remained and left the shelter of the trees. "There it is!" He pointed to the strange shape of the hill that showed up more clearly in the morning sun. "It shouldn't take us long to get there."

In fact it was further away than it looked, and the sun was quite high in the sky by the time the dragons landed on a grassy hummock at the foot of the hill. There were two small leaning rowan trees and a big bush of gorse, just bursting into flower, in between them. At each side of the trees were two outcrops of brownish rock exactly the same size and shape. Above them the hillside rose in a sheer cliff, impossible to climb, even with four legs. It looked as though there was a flat ledge above the cliff. Leaving the others to rest beside the rocks, Dad took a flying leap and landed on the ledge. In a moment his head appeared over the edge.

"There's quite a big space here," he said. "Come up."

There was plenty of room on the ledge for all of them, even though there were ridges of curious lumpy grey rock lying about. Again the cliff behind was sheer but from this point they could see the smooth round top of the hill. There was a ring of untidy grass round the edge of it, and various lumps of rock jutted out. Tom pointed in excitement.

"There *is* a cave!" he shouted. "Look, up there there's a hole in the rock. I bet we could squeeze in there. Can I fly up and see?"

"That wouldn't be any good to us," said Mum. "There's nowhere to land outside it. It's just a cave in the air! I don't think this place will do. It doesn't feel like an ordinary mountain to me. I don't like it. There's a strange noise too—can you hear it?"

They all listened quietly, and heard a regular sighing sound. Mum shivered. "Creepy!" she said.

"Just the wind," said Dad briskly. "Why don't we land on the very top? Then we can look all around and see if there are any better places. I'll check inside that cave on the way up."

They took off again, circled the ledge and flew up to the smooth summit. It was slippery but big enough for all of them. Dad hovered for a minute outside the round cave and then joined them.

"No good," he said, "far too small and full of sharp white stalactites. But we have a great view from up here, so let's look round carefully." He scanned the slopes of the mountain behind them, but it was disappointingly smooth and grassy. Mum was still looking tense and worried. Tom climbed down the side a little way and perched precariously on one of the sticking out rocks.

"Tom, be careful, you'll fall!" she said.

Tom laughed. "Mu-u-um! I can *fly* you know! Anyone would think I was a hatchling!"

"Sorry," said Mum. "Of course you can. It's this place getting on my nerves. It doesn't feel safe."

Emily had been staring out at the wide country in front of her. Below them a small river looped around the hill and flowed down a steep valley and out of sight. Across the river she could see trees, grassy glades and the edge of a loch. Miles and miles of beautiful wild country stretched into the misty

47

distance. "No sign of any other dragons, but I'd like to live here. If only there was a cave!" she sighed, then lay on her front and peered down to the lower ledge. Suddenly she gave a little scream. "Look!" she said.

Mum and Dad came over, and Tom leaned from his perch on the rock and stared too. Emily pointed down.

"See those rocks?" she said. "They look exactly like two long talons lying there. You can see them properly from up here."

"You and your imagination!" said Dad.

"I think she's right," said Mum. "I think we should go! It's dangerous here. It feels wrong." She leaned down, huffing thoughtfully.

As she did so a shiver ran through the mountain. At the same moment Tom shouted, "My rock's wobbling!" and they all felt the hill beneath them shake. They huffed in alarm, their combined smoke poured down the hill and suddenly there was a sound like an explosion followed by a violent earthquake.

"Fly!" shouted Dad. "And keep together!"

They flew up and away in fright, but before they had gone far, Emily turned, looked back and screamed. Two enormous eyes had appeared on the front of the hilltop.

The eyes stared alarmingly, then blinked slowly. "Well I never!" said a deep voice. "Four little dragons! Steady there. I feel another sneeze coming on. AAA-TISHOO!!!"

The four dragons were buffeted and birled like flies in the rush of air. As the noise subsided, they landed in a tangled heap of wings and tails at the foot of the mountain, stunned and breathing heavily.

When they had picked themselves up, they stared at the hill. From this angle it was plain to see what it was; feet, knees, hands, a bald head with a fringe of hair. Ears, nose, mouth . . .

"It's a giant! A real live giant!" Emily breathed.

"I sat on his ear," Tom whispered in a trembling voice.

"I peered into his mouth!" said Dad.

"I *knew* there was something strange about this place," said Mum. "We'd better get away while we still can. Come on! Are you kids fit to fly?" They tried to spread crumpled and shaking wings.

"No cause for alarm," said the voice like a deep rumble of thunder. "I haven't seen a dragon for centuries. I always liked dragons in the old days. Ben McIlwhinnie's the name."

Chapter 8

Ben McIlwhinnie Helps Out

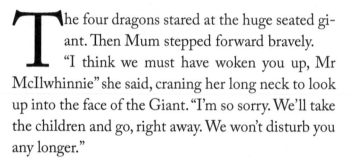

The four dragons stared at the huge seated giant. Then Mum stepped forward bravely.

"I think we must have woken you up, Mr McIlwhinnie" she said, craning her long neck to look up into the face of the Giant. "I'm so sorry. We'll take the children and go, right away. We won't disturb you any longer."

"Please, please, I beg you, stay!" said the Giant. "It's so long since I had the chance to talk with dragons. And I can see that you are blue *Scottish* dragons too, which makes you even more welcome. Tell me, did you huff smoke past my nose?" They all nodded. "Ah, that explains the sneezes. And I think I felt something tickling my left ear?"

"That was me," admitted Tom, looking scared. "I was sitting on it. Sorry."

"Of course you were," beamed the Giant. "A perfect perch for a dragonlet! What are your names?"

Dad introduced them all, "Gwen, Emily, Tom, and I'm Duncan," and the Giant smiled at each in turn. "I am delighted to meet you. But what are you doing in this part of the country? Why don't you fly up and sit on my knee so that we can chat in comfort. Perch on my fingers."

"I think we'll be safe," whispered Mum cautiously, and they all flew up to the second ledge and settled down on the spreading rocky fingers of Ben McIllwhinnie. Dad began their story.

"We come from a cave over there," he said, waving a claw in the vague direction from which they had come. "We've lived there for years, since before the children hatched. But we've just discovered that Humans are starting to build in our glen so we can't stay."

"Of course you can't!" the Giant interrupted in horror. "A plague of Humans is enough to drive any peace-loving dragon away. How did you find out?"

"We went down two nights ago and found a sign with writing on. Emily read it. I always said that reading of hers would come in useful."

"No you didn't, you always said it was a waste of time!" Mum interrupted, and the giant chuckled, a deep rumble that shook them all. Tom rolled over, giggling, quite forgetting his fright.

"Well done young Emily! So you need to move, and you would like to live here, is that what you are suggesting?"

"It would be lovely," said Mum. "But you wouldn't want a noisy family disturbing your peace. And we need a cave—quite a big one."

"My dear Mistress Gwen, I shall be asleep again in a day or so, and I may not wake again for centuries," exclaimed the Giant. "I would be delighted to have a family of dragons keeping watch on my hill. And as for a cave, there's one right beneath us. Did you not see it as you came up? I don't think it's occupied at present and I think you would find it sufficiently spacious. Go and see."

Mum and Dad looked at each other in amazement, but Emily and Tom bounced off the Giant's knee in excitement and disappeared onto the lower ledge. There was no sign of a cave. Then Emily had an idea. She wriggled round the edge of the big gorse bush in the middle and shouted with excitement. Hidden behind it was the entrance to a cave under the rock that formed the Giant's armchair. Tom came behind her.

"Mum! Dad! Come and look!" he shouted, and tried to push past Emily to get inside.

"Wait a minute," said Dad, flying down. "I'm going in first. You can't be too careful in strange caves."

He stepped gingerly through the opening and sent a huff of flame ahead of him to light up the inside. Two tiny weasels shot between his legs and made off at speed down the hill, but otherwise the cave seemed to be empty. "Come inside," he said. "This looks just right!"

Emily came next and looked around. Inside the entrance the roof was quite high, and she could see three or four openings at the back, so there might be inner caves, which would be *very* useful. Perhaps she could have a bedroom to herself! The floor was smooth but the walls had ledges and ridges and there were little shiny stalactites hanging from the roof, though it seemed quite dry at the moment. Tom pushed his way into one of the inner caves and came out in a hurry.

"There's a pile of bones in there," he said and dived into the next chamber. "And heaps of old poo in this one, Emily!" he yelled.

"Yuk! You can have that one!"

"You'd expect a few bones in an ancient cave," Dad said, peering into each opening. "Tom, don't jump in that, even if it has dried up!"

"I don't think anyone has lived in here for a long time. That gorse bush grew and hid the entrance a long time ago," said Mum.

"That means Mr McIlwhinnie must have been asleep for *ages*," said Emily. "He didn't know about the gorse. Do you think the rowan trees have grown up since he was last awake as well? I'll ask him. He must be very, very old."

"Don't be too nosey," warned Mum. "We don't want him to change his mind about dragon neighbours. I think this cave is just what we want, but there are things to check out first. Children, leave the talking to us."

They made their way back up to the Giant's knee. "Well, did you find it?" he said. "Will it do? I think one time I was awake there were a couple of bears hibernating in it, but that must have been quite a while ago."

"Ages ago!" said Emily. "My books say that bears stopped living in Scotland centuries back."

The giant's eyes twinkled at her. "Ah, but I expect Humans think *dragons* are extinct in Scotland too," he said. "And we know they're wrong! When would you like to move in?"

"There is one problem," said Mum. "We'll need a fire for cooking outside the cave. Won't the smoke make you sneeze again? You won't want us waking you up all the time!"

"Oh, I wouldn't worry about that! Your little fire beside my feet won't trouble me. The smoke will blow away long before it reaches my nose. Your fires will ward off chilblains in the winter. And however much noise you make, it won't sound loud to *me* when I'm asleep. As long as you young dragonlets promise not to huff up my nostrils as a joke, we should get along very well."

"Then thank you very much, Mr McIlwhinnie, we'd love to move in," said Dad, after Mum had nodded her agreement. He smiled at the beaming faces of his children. "We'll all fly back home and start packing up right away." He reached out a claw and solemnly shook one of the giant's fingers.

"Call me Ben—it means 'mountain' as I expect you know, so it's a very good name for someone as big as me."

"Dad," Emily interrupted, "it might not be safe to go back. What if those Humans have found the cave?"

"A good point, young Emily," said Ben. "I would advise you go straight away, and fly back overnight. Why don't you leave your dragonlets with me? It's a long way for them to fly, and you'll be safer without them."

"YES!" shouted Emily and Tom, for once in full agreement. Tom thought it was the perfect chance for a bit of private exploration, while Emily was fascinated by Ben McIlwhinnie and wanted to talk to him before he fell asleep again. She had a feeling he would be even better than a book!

"Are you sure?" Mum asked dubiously, looking first at her children and then at Ben.

"YES!"

"Quite sure," said Ben. "Nothing will harm them while I'm awake. They can sleep up here in the shelter of my fingers. You two should be able to see off any Humans if you don't have your dragonlets to worry about. And I have a feeling you youngsters might enjoy a little time to yourselves." He gave them a knowing look with his twinkly eyes which Emily wondered about, though Tom was giggling too much at the idea that his parents might be called 'youngsters' to notice.

"We'll be back as soon as we can tomorrow morning," said Dad. "We'll leave you the rest of the food, so if you're sure you'll be all right . . .?" He rather liked Ben's idea.

"We'll be fine. I'll look after Tom," said Emily. (Tom said "Huh!" under his breath but nobody was listening.) "You will be careful, won't you? If Humans have found the cave, they might be waiting to ambush you," she added anxiously.

"You and your stories! Mum and I will be quite safe, don't worry."

"If you spread your wings I'll give you a good strong blow to speed you on your way," said Ben, and in a few minutes, Mum and Dad were tiny specks in the blue sky and Emily and Tom were on their own with Ben.

Chapter 9

Monsters in the Loch

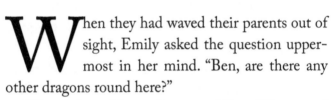

When they had waved their parents out of sight, Emily asked the question uppermost in her mind. "Ben, are there any other dragons round here?"

"Not as far as I know," answered Ben. "There used to be several big ones in these mountains, but that must have been centuries ago. I wouldn't worry if I were you. I don't think they'll be here now."

"But I'd *like* to have other dragons around! It would be lovely to have some friends."

"Can we fly down through the woods to the loch?" Tom interrupted.

Ben nodded his huge head. "You'll come to no harm over there, but be back before it begins to get dark. I don't want to have to come and find you. Rising to my feet is such an effort these days."

"We will," said Emily, who was as keen to explore as Tom. "I want to be back in time to ask him for a bedtime story," she explained as they headed for the trees. When they reached the edge of the wood, she turned and waved to Ben, who lifted a huge hand in reply. Several black crows flying near shot off in the opposite direction in alarm, and the children chuckled.

"What would happen if he *did* get to his feet?" Emily wondered. "Would our new cave collapse?"

"Never mind that," said Tom impatiently. "Come *on*!"

They made their way quietly through the wood. The trees were not pine, like the wood near their old cave, but a mix of larch, rowan, elder and oak, with strange twisted branches and new leaves shining in the sunlight. The grass under their feet was dotted with wild flowers and there were clumps of primroses under the trees. The air seemed full of insects and small birds. They followed a faint path, probably made by deer, and soon came to the shores of the loch near the place where the little river flowed in. It was a long narrow loch and the trees grew right to the water's edge on this side.

Tom was just wondering whether Emily would let him try a swim when they both saw something strange in the water. A long dark humped shape was appearing and disappearing on the surface not far away, swimming fast. Then with a flurry it vanished. They stared in horror.

"W- what was that?" Tom whispered.

"I don't know," said Emily, "but I've read about a monster that lives in a loch, and it's supposed to look like that when it swims along."

As they watched, the shape reappeared, much nearer, heading towards them. This time they could see a head with big eyes and short bristly whiskers. It held a sizeable fish in its mouth. The creature swam to a rock a little further along the shore, climbed out of the water on short legs and shook water drops off a long body and tail. It dropped the fish, planting a paw firmly on it as it flapped feebly, and stared at the dragons in surprise. A minute later, a second creature swam up to the rock, and reared up on its hind legs to stare too. It looked tall and fierce and opened a mouth full of sharp teeth. That was too much for the young dragons, and they fled back into the shelter of the trees. A loud barking sound echoed after them.

"What were they?" Tom asked again. "They didn't look friendly! They eat fish like we do. Do you think they huff flames as well?"

"They looked a *bit* like us," said Emily. "Long tails anyway. Furry, I think, though it was difficult to tell when they were all wet and shiny. No wings or spikes. I've never seen anything like them before. Let's go back and ask Ben."

They hurried up the hill, trying not to run, half expecting the strange creatures to follow them.

'When they got back in sight of Ben, the huge eyes were shut.

"Oh no!" said Tom, "he's gone back to sleep. What shall we do?"

"I don't know," said Emily dreamily. "He really is magic, isn't he? When his eyes are open you can tell he's a giant, but now he looks just like a mountain again."

"That's no help!" said Tom in exasperation as they came closer. "BEN! WAKE UP!" he yelled as loudly as he could.

"Just dozing," came Ben's rumbling voice. "Well, what did you find in your explorations?" He made the word sound very important, and his eyes opened and twinkled at Emily. She had the feeling that he could

read her thoughts, and knew all about the adventure stories she loved so much. "Climb on my hand so we can talk without you two having to shout."

Puzzled, the little dragons flew up to Ben's knee, and found that the long rocky fingers on one side had turned over, so that Ben's enormous hand, palm upwards, rested lightly on his knees. There was a scatter of moss, earth and uprooted weeds around it—which proved how long Ben had been asleep, Emily thought. It was as if his hand had become part of the hill! She and Tom climbed on; there was plenty of room.

"Hold tight!" said Ben, and the dragons giggled with delight as the hand rose slowly into the air until it was on a level with Ben's face. "Now then, tell me all about it."

Tom started to tell about the creatures in the loch. He made them sound significantly bigger and fiercer, Emily thought, so perhaps he was a bit ashamed of running away. She added a few details herself, and Ben nodded his head. "The Otters," he said, "delightful creatures. Far better neighbours than Humans, you'll find. They have always lived around this loch. I expect those two have cubs in their holt somewhere, though they will be very young so early in the spring."

"What's a *holt*?"

"A cave for otters to live in, close to the water. They spend most of their time in the water, but they come ashore to play. If I were you, I'd go and make friends as soon as you've settled in. Did you like my woods?"

"Oh, yes," said Emily, "*much* nicer than the woods near our old cave, where the trees were all the same, and always a boring dark green. These look much more *alive* somehow, and there are far more birds."

"Humans again!" said Ben sadly. "They planted pine trees all over the hills, for some reason. But they don't come near this glen, so these trees and the otters are quite safe."

"Why not?" asked Tom.

"Ah, that's a long story, and better kept for later," said Ben. "I'll put you down now, and you can have some supper, and then I'll tell you more about my glen before you go to bed." He slowly lowered his hand.

Emily proudly huffed her first proper fire to heat up their supper. She was looking forward to a bedtime story with their new friend.

Chapter 10

A Tale of Long Ago

There wasn't quite enough food left, and Emily generously let Tom eat more than his fair share, since he always made a fuss when he was hungry. The left-over food was mainly snails, but fortunately she found four crumbly bramble biscuits at the very bottom of the bag. She hoped their parents wouldn't be too late bringing supplies next morning. She wondered how they were getting on, and hoped they hadn't found any Humans lying in wait with swords or bows and arrows.

When they had finished and she and Tom had washed their faces and cleaned their teeth, she asked Ben for the promised story, hoping to hear why he disliked Humans so much.

"Make yourselves comfortable first," he said, and curling his hand he made a cosy shelter for them to sleep in. His thumb made a good roof, so it almost felt like a cave, and the scattered moss was comfy to lie on. They couldn't see his face, but his low rumbling voice was very comforting and they felt safe and happy.

"Many many years ago, when I was younger, I spent more time awake," he began. "My eyes were sharper then, and I could see far down the valley; as far as the distant mountains. There is one craggy outcrop of rock down there, and I awoke one year to find dozens of men with horses and rocks and ropes, building a castle on the top. The ruins are still there, I believe."

"I saw it!" Emily exclaimed. "When I looked out at the view just before you woke up, I spotted a crag with strange jagged shapes on top. I wondered what it was. Then you sneezed, and I forgot about it."

"Young eyes, you see! Yes, that will be what is left of the castle. It was huge when they had finished it, and commanded a fine view up and down the wide river valley. But I was not worried, because it was far away, and I went back to sleep.

"It must have been many years later when I next woke to hear horrible sounds. A mighty battle was in progress, the castle was battered by great machines, dead men and horses lay scattered all around and the crows and ravens were gathering. For hours the battle raged, and in the night I could see flames rising from the castle hill. When the dawn rose the next day, the castle was a black smouldering ruin and the few men who remained were mustering to ride their horses down the valley. The carrion birds were feasting on the bodies of the dead. Until then I did not believe that Humans could kill their own kind for no good reason. There is land enough for all, food and water in plenty in these hills. Why kill so many for a single crag in a valley! Why destroy the work of so many builders in a single night?"

Ben fell silent, and the children did not like to ask questions. Emily was picturing the horrible scene in her mind. Eventually she spoke. "Did you ever find out why they had the battle?"

"Yes I did, though I never understood it. Three days later, when the fire had died to a faint glow in the night, I was still watching and thinking, too disturbed to go back to sleep, when I saw a man leading two weary horses climbing up from the loch. Slumped on one of the horses was another man, swaying as he came. They saw your cave and took shelter, built a small fire, tethered their horses and settled for the night. They did not notice me in the gloaming.

"The next morning the man carried the body of his friend over his shoulder to the bottom of the hill, dug a pit and buried him. He stood awhile with his head bowed, then turned to climb back, and that is when he spotted me and recognised what I was."

"Just like we did!" said Tom. "We must have landed on the very same spot."

"Ssshh," said Emily.

"I waited for him to flee in fear," Ben continued. "But he bowed and spoke with great reverence, as though I was someone to be worshipped, and not just plain Ben McIlwhinnie! I told him I meant him no harm and we talked throughout that day. His name was Donald. He had been born and raised in these hills but was forced by his clan chief to leave his village and his family to fight in the battle. Two clan leaders were fighting over the castle, and now it was destroyed and worthless, and many men lay dead. The friend he had just buried had been wounded and he had not been able to save his life. He was very sad. He said he would return to his village and trouble me no longer, and the next morning he rode away, leading his friend's horse. He was a good man. Not all Humans are bad."

"I do hope he got back safely to his family," said Emily. "I don't suppose you ever saw him again."

"Oh, but I did! One day I woke to hear my name shouted over and over. There, beside my feet, was an old, old man. It was Donald, grown old as I slept. He sat on my hand, as you did, and told of his long life, of his home with his wife, of his children and their children, of their land and crops and cattle. He fought no more battles, but he never forgot Ben McIlwhinnie who guarded the grave of his friend. Now his wife was dead, his children settled with their families and well able to tend his beloved land, and so he had travelled south to visit me once more. And he told me that he had spread rumours of a haunted mountain near the site of the battle, so no-one would come and disturb my peaceful glen. The next morning, I found that Donald had died peacefully in his sleep. I dug a grave with my finger and buried him under my left hand, and here his bones remain."

Emily felt Tom shiver beside her. "It's all right," she whispered. "It was a very long time ago. And Ben said he was a good man." Raising her voice she asked, "Is that why you said we'd be safe from Humans here?"

"Yes. Centuries have past, and I think Humans are less superstitious these days, but the peace of this glen remains. They still keep away."

"Do you *really* not mind if we come to live here?" Emily asked anxiously.

"No, I like dragons. You only kill when you need to eat, and you seldom fight each other." (Tom and Emily looked at each other a little guiltily when he said this.) "I have never heard of a dragon who forced other dragons to fight on his behalf like that clan chief! I know you huff flames when you're bigger, but when you've finished with a fire you always jump it out, don't you? Believe me, that's very important with all this bracken around. Humans are far too careless with fires! Now I think you should settle down for the night. Sleep well, little dragonlets!"

Tom and Emily snuggled together in the shelter of Ben's hand. Tom soon fell asleep, but Emily wanted to stay awake to think about Ben's story. For a while she stared up at the moon, thinking of the great battle and their glen, protected by Donald's legend, until she fell asleep too. Neither of them stirred until the sun was up the next morning, and they were woken by the beating of dragon wings as their parents returned.

Chapter 11

Settling In

Emily and Tom crawled from their bed and stretched their wings in the sun. "Hello!" said Emily happily. "I'm so glad you're back safely. Did you see any Humans? I've been a bit worried."

"No sign of them," said Dad. "Hopefully that man had forgotten he'd seen us by the time he woke up."

"No-one would believe him," rumbled Ben's voice from above. "Everybody knows dragons don't exist!"

"I'm hungry!" said Tom. "We've had a great time but you didn't leave us nearly enough food."

"We thought you might be in need of a good breakfast," said Mum. "So we'll have that first, before we start cleaning out the cave and settling in."

Breakfast took quite a time, but finally even Tom was full. Ben had been invited to share their food but, rather to Mum's relief, he said he didn't eat much these days. He confessed he was enjoying the smell of the cooking and the warmth on his toes, so he would try to stay awake for a bit longer.

Emily and Tom looked at the pile of things that had been brought from the old cave, and wondered if it would all fit inside.

"Cleaning first," said Mum briskly. "I'll light a torch so we can see what we're doing. Start at the far end. Come on!"

Tom tried to make poo-bombs to throw at the others, but to his disappointment the pile crumbled to dust and was swept outside. They set to work with tails and twiggy brooms and swept all the inner chambers clean. There were three of a reasonable size plus the one with the bones, which was smaller. After some discussion, they decided to leave the bones undisturbed. Emily was pleased. She was still thinking of the story Ben had told her about the two graves on the hill, and wondered what creature had died and left its bones in the cave.

"Do you two want a room each?" asked Mum. "Dad and I are having this one."

"Yes please!" said Emily, delighted.

"Well, let's make a rule," said Dad, "you keep your own rooms clean and tidy, and you make your own beds. Agreed?"

"Yes."

"I want the Poo Cave, and nobody is allowed in unless I say," Tom added.

"Let's start now," said Mum. "We need lots of dry bracken and heather. Off you go."

While Emily and Tom flew to and fro with bundles for three beds, Dad carried their things into the cave and Mum arranged them. It looked very cosy and home-like when they had finished. Emily had rescued her books from the pile, and was pleased to find that her room had a little rock shelf that she could keep them on. She arranged her bed neatly, lay down on it to check that it was comfy, and sent a happy huff up to the roof. There was a chorus of high squeaks, and three small bats wriggled from a crack in the roof and peered down at her disapprovingly.

"Sorry, I didn't mean to wake you up," she said. "I'm Emily, and I've just moved in. But I won't get in your way, I promise. I'll try not to huff while you're asleep." The bats squeaked and shuffled back into their crevice and Emily crept into the living room.

"I've got bats," she announced.

"Will they bother you?" asked Dad. "We can huff them out if you don't want them." He carried another pile of firewood into the bone cave, where he was storing it out of the way, carefully avoiding the bones.

"That wouldn't be fair. They were here first! I don't mind sharing," said Emily.

"If they make a mess, they'll have to go," said Mum, who was putting food on rock ledges, "but they can stay for now. Do you want a drink?"

"Yes, please," said Tom, coming hurriedly out of his private cave. "And a bumblebug?" he added hopefully. "We've worked really hard!"

"Here you are," said Mum, "two each. Then you can go out and amuse yourselves while I finish organising in here."

"Can we take Dad down to the loch?" Tom asked. "I want to see if those big swimming beasties are still there."

"Otters," Emily corrected him, "I want to see them too."

"I'll finish stacking this wood and follow you down," said Dad. "I've seen otters before and they're quite harmless, unless you're a fish."

"D'you think they can talk?" Tom asked as they set off.

"Ben said they were friendly," Emily said. "I hope they are. I expect we'll soon find out!"

Chapter 12

The New Neighbours

They didn't hurry through the wood, because they both secretly hoped Dad would catch them up before they got to the loch. Instead they explored sideways from the path, listened to the drumming of a woodpecker high in a tree, chased three rabbits back to their burrows and scythed a patch of nettles with their tails. When they saw Dad flying overhead a few minutes later, they hurried to join him on the loch-side.

"What a wonderful loch!" said Dad enthusiastically. "Much nearer home for fishing, unless those otters of yours have taken them all. I can't see them, can you?"

"There!" said Emily, pointing up the loch with one claw, and sure enough, two round heads could be seen in the distance. Dad sent up a smoke huff, and within seconds the heads surfaced close to where they were standing and stared at them suspiciously.

"Wow, they *are* fast swimmers!" Tom whispered enviously.

"Hello!" Dad called. "We're the Dragons. We've just moved in to Ben McIlwhinnie's cave. I hope you don't mind if we share your loch. How's the fishing?"

The otters swam to the shallows beside them and paddled ashore, giving themselves their usual hearty shake so that water drops showered over Tom and Emily. They seemed smaller now that Dad was with them and not fierce at all. Both young dragons felt ashamed of their flight the day before.

"Fishin's great," said the first otter. "D'ye eat fish? Are ye aa' plannin' on stayin' like?"

"Yes," said Dad. "We eat lots of other things as well," he added hurriedly as the two otters looked at each other with worried expressions. "We wouldn't want to steal your food. There should be plenty in a loch this size, surely!"

The otters relaxed a little. "Aye," said the second one, "there should be enough for us a', tho' we've two growin' bairns in the holt, and they eat a lot. Is there jist the three o' ye?"

"There's Mum as well," said Emily. "I'm Emily and this is Tom. Ben said you would have little ones—bairns I mean. Can we see them? Are they old enough to play with?"

The female otter smiled, "Aye, I'll give them a call now we ken ye're friendly. No puffin' flames out when you're playing with them, mind!"

"Course not!" said Emily. "Tom's too young for flames anyway." Tom scowled at her, but she ignored him. "Please call them!"

The otter stood up high and sent out a series of short barking calls. A minute later there was a splashing flurry across the loch and two little otters scrambled out of the water and tumbled in a wet heap on the grass, shouting cheerfully. "Ah won!" "Naw, ye didnae!" They rolled over and over and it was difficult to see which was which, until their dad separated them by the scruff of their necks and sat them side by side on the grass. They looked exactly alike, with round faces, big eyes and identical whiskery grins.

"Lottie and Wattie," said their father, proudly. "Right wee tearaways!"

"These're the Dragons," said their mother. "They've come to bide on Ben's Hill."

"Can ye swim?" asked Wattie (or maybe Lottie, Emily wasn't sure which was which.) "Race ye across?"

"Course we can. Bet you can't fly!" said Tom, determined not to be outdone. He had a feeling he would lose a swimming race.

"Don't start!" said Mum, appearing behind them out of the trees. "Hallo," she added politely to the Otter family. "I do hope these three haven't disturbed your fishing."

"Na, na, plenty space roond here and plenty o' fish fer us aa'. The bairns can play th'gither. Yours willna' droon, will they?"

"Not if they're careful," said Mum. "Don't go too deep to start with, and remember you need to shake your wings dry before you try to fly," she told her children.

"Will you be all right if Mum and I fly down the loch for a look around?" asked Dad.

"Course we will!"

"Keep an eye oot fer the Ospreys. They fish here times, tho' Ah doubt they'll bother a couple o' dragons," said the otter. "No showin' off, mind!" he added sternly to his cubs as he and his wife dived and swam away.

While their parents enjoyed a soaring flight to the far end of the loch and a little way down the valley, Emily and Tom had a swimming lesson with the two otter cubs. Tom loved the water and soon found that he could flap his wings underwater and get along quite well. The little otters swam over and under him, encouraging him to go faster. He tried an underwater somersault, and Emily was startled when his bright blue tail appeared, sticking straight out of the water and waving wildly. Lottie and Wattie cheered.

"Ha' a shot!" they shouted to Emily, but she shook her head. There was no way she was standing on her head under water! She was suddenly feeling rather lonely.

Chapter 13

Emily's Plan

Emily steered herself away from the rumpus created by Tom and the cubs and paddled slowly along on the surface close to the shore. She had a lovely view of coots' and moorhens' nests in the reeds and thought how nice it would be if she had a friend who would paddle quietly along beside her.

When she turned round to head back, she was surprised how far she had travelled. Her legs were beginning to feel quite tired. Tom was jumping excitedly in the shallows, shouting, "Mum, Dad, look what I can do!" and, glancing up, Emily saw her parents coming in to land on the bank. Mum waved to her while Dad watched Tom demonstrate his underwater head-stand and tail-waving trick. "Emily can't swim as well as me!" he boasted to Dad as he surfaced, spluttering.

Mum came to meet her. "You went a long way," she said. "Are you enjoying it?"

"I don't like putting my head in the water," Emily confessed quietly so that Tom wouldn't hear. "So I can't swim with the otters, like Tom. It was lovely and peaceful along there though. I don't *really* mind being on my own."

Her mother smiled sympathetically. "Come back to the cave with me," she said. "Dad can stay with Tom. We'll come down tomorrow morning by ourselves and have a quiet swimming lesson."

"Those otters are far too good at it," said Emily. "But they can't fly! I think I like flying better." As she and Mum took off and circled over the loch before heading back to the cave she did a quick loop-the-loop, just to show off to the cubs. They stood up on a rock and waved before diving back into the water.

"The little otters are fun," she said as they were lighting the fire for an early supper, "but it's still not like having a *real* friend. Do you think there might be other dragons near here? I asked Ben, but he didn't think so." She sighed heavily.

"We could try some signalling perhaps," said Mum thoughtfully. "You practise your huffing on this fire and we'll see what Dad says tomorrow. I think we need a good night's sleep in our new bedrooms first. It's been an exciting couple of days." She gave Emily a sympathetic pat and went into the cave.

"Signalling?" thought Emily as she huffed. "I wonder what that means. . . ."

When the fire was burning steadily under a pot of crow stew, she flew to the top of Ben's head and peered down. "Ben?" she called quietly.

Ben's big eyes opened and looked up at her. "What can I do for you, young Emily?" he asked. "Do I get the impression that you're not *quite* satisfied with your new home?"

"Oh I am! I love the cave and the woods and the loch! But it's a bit lonely. Tom is quite happy with the little otters, but I'd LOVE a dragon friend. I've always wanted someone to have adventures with. Do you think I'll ever find a friend?"

"Hmm, difficult to say," said Ben. "You can keep an eye out for one flying over, perhaps."

"I always do, but I've never ever seen one! Mum said something about signalling, but I don't know what she means."

"Ah, signalling! Just like the old days. Beacons and smoke on every hilltop! Worth a try, Emily, worth a try..." His eyes closed and Emily sighed. It didn't look as though Ben would be much help in this new quest.

She was about to go back to the fire when she saw Dad flying up from the loch hustling along a dripping Tom. Mum called Tom down to get dry before supper, but Dad carried on up the hill and landed beside Emily.

"What a wonderful place!" he said happily gazing around. "It couldn't have worked out better! What a good thing you spotted those yellow dragons when you did. Well done Emily!"

"Thanks," said Emily, with a very tiny sigh. Dad heard it and looked at her thoughtfully.

"And this is a perfect spot for a signal station," he said, putting a wing round her. "I know, Emily—you want a friend. You've talked about it often enough. Well, tomorrow we'll have a try at signalling from here. It's a good deal higher than the old cave. Let's see if we can contact some other dragons. I'll teach you all about the Gloaming Huff. I don't think Ben will mind."

"Not at all, not at all," rumbled the voice from below, sleepily. "If anyone deserves to succeed in her quest, it's your clever young Emily!"

Three huffs from below told them that supper was ready.

"Thank you, Dad! Thank you, Ben!" Emily danced with excitement in mid air, twirling her tail and waving her wings, and Mum and Tom looked up and applauded. The bats emerged from their cave and joined in, squeaking and waggling their wings before flying off in the gathering dusk for a night's hunting. Then she followed Dad down to the ledge between Ben's huge feet for a special celebration supper outside their new home.

END OF BOOK ONE

Will Emily ever find her Dragon friend?

Her search brings Desmond, a strange and colourful Traveller, who takes the family on an adventurous journey.

Emily gets her wish, Tom gets a fright and finds a hero, and there are plenty of surprises in store for all of the family.

Share Emily and Tom's adventures in *Dragon Tales Book 2: Quest for a Friend* by Judy Hayman.

Coming late 2014.

Acknowledgements

To all my family, who have given such support and encouragement, and especially Peter for much-needed technical help and my editorial and design committee, granddaughters Phoebe and Elise.

And to Alison Jones, whose friendship and professional expertise brought these books to publication; Margaret Forrester whose books inspired me; Margaret and Gordon Liddell who advised on dragon food and otter-speak; Ettie Spencer and Lydia Macdonald, who found me Caroline, who brought the dragons to life.

About the author

 Judy Hayman lives with her husband Peter on the edge of the Lammermuir Hills in East Lothian, where there is a wonderful view and plenty of wildlife, but no dragons, as far as she knows. At various times in her past life she has been an English teacher in a big comprehensive school; a playwright, director and occasionally actor with amateur theatre companies; a Parliamentary candidate for both Westminster and the Scottish Parliament; and a Mum. Sometimes all at once. Now preventing the Lammermuirs from taking over her garden and being a Gran takes up a lot of time, and fits well with writing these Dragon Tales.

About the illustrator

 Caroline Wolfe Murray studied Archaeology at the University of Edinburgh and took a career path in the field, turning her hand to archaeological illustration. She has always had a passion for exploration and discovery which evolved from her experience of living in Spain, Belgium, Venezuela and New Zealand. She now resides in East Lothian with her husband James and her two young daughters Lily and Mabel, who have been her inspiration to work on a children's book.

Enjoy Dragon Tales Book 1? Read on for the first chapter of Dragon Tales Book 2: Quest for a Friend, coming late 2014...

Chapter 1

The Gloaming Huff

Emily the young dragon sat on the top of Ben McIlwhinnie's bald head at the end of a fine evening. Ben was a Scottish Mountain Giant, and the top of his head made an excellent lookout point. From here, Emily could look down the remote Highland glen to the loch, half hidden with trees and bushes, and the far-distant hills. It was wild and lonely with no sign of Humans anywhere, and Emily loved it.

It was the shock discovery that Humans were moving into their old glen that had forced the family to move. Emily shivered as she remembered the spooky night flight with her father when they had found a horrible wire fence, huge machines and even a nasty square building with a real live Human inside. "Thank goodness we've got wings!" she thought, remembering their escape.

But now they had discovered Ben, and the cave under his huge rocky chair. She and her parents and younger brother Tom had found a safe new home.

The family had had a busy week; settling into the new cave, exploring the moorland leading up the mountains, foraging in the woods and swimming in the nearby loch with their new friends, the Otters. They were all delighted with their new home. Ben had gone back to sleep now, but he had made them promise to wake him up if anything important happened. "Good things or dangerous things, I don't mind which. A good strong huff should do it," he had said. Now Emily could hear the soft sighing of his breathing, sounding just like the wind. It reminded her that he was always there if she needed him.

She knew that Tom was quite content with his new life. He loved swimming with Lottie and Wattie, the young otter cubs, and spent as much time as he was allowed down at the loch diving and wallowing with a lot of noise. Emily wasn't such a good swimmer, but Mum had patiently coaxed her underwater, and although she was still not as confident as Tom, she was getting better at opening her eyes under the surface. She was fascinated by the teeming life in the loch, though the first time she had come nose to nose with a large trout she was startled into swallowing rather a lot of water. All the serious fishing had to be done at the other end of the loch these days, and the local Ospreys had given up in disgust and flown to a different one.

She loved having a cave to herself at night, and spent a lot of time reading or making plans and dreaming. She was quite friendly with the bats in her roof, though they were usually back in bed by the time she woke up in the morning, so they didn't really count as the kind of friends she needed.

Finding other dragons had become the most important thing to Emily. She thought of it as her New Quest, which sounded grand and as adventurous as her favourite stories. So she was very excited when she had learned about the Gloaming Huff.

After supper one night Dad had explained all about it.

"Mum and I never bothered back at our old cave," he had said, "but I know you'd like to see if there are other dragons around. Why not? This cave is higher than our old one, so it might be a good place for the Gloaming Huff."

"What's that?" Emily had asked, puzzled.

"Well, you know we often use smoke signalling," Dad had explained. "This is much the same, but you only do it in the evening. You go to the top of a hill and send a steady huff of smoke as high as you can, for as long as you can. Then you look all around to see if you can spot any other smoke. That's the Gloaming Huff. It's an ancient method of communication between dragons, and it's one that Humans don't notice, for some reason. There's quite a complicated code, so you can send messages once you've made contact with another dragon. We could try if you like. You never know, some other dragon might spot our signal."

"Oh, please let's try!" Emily had exclaimed. So for the next three evenings, she and Dad had flown to the top of Ben's head and Dad had sent a straight huff high into the air. Then they had waited hopefully, gazing all around, until the light faded and it was Emily's bedtime. But there had been no answering smoke. Dad had decided it was a waste of time trying again, but Mum, who realised how disappointed Emily was, persuaded him to have one more Huff. This time, she and Dad huffed together, so their plume was higher and lasted longer, and Emily huffed too, just to feel she was helping.

Then Mum and Dad had gone back to the cave to make sure Tom cleaned his teeth before bed, but had allowed Emily to stay for a few more minutes, just in case.

"Any minute they'll call me down," she thought, "and it hasn't worked. I'll never find a friend!" She heaved a heavy sigh and then stood up as high as she could for a last look round. And then she saw it: a thin plume of white smoke far away to the south, just visible against the deepening blue of the evening sky.

"Dad, Dad!" she shouted. "Come quick! I've seen one!"

Both her parents flew up straight away and looked for the smoke. "Well spotted, Emily!" said Mum. "It's a long way away, but we must send an answer." She and Dad sent first a steady stream, and then a series of puffs.

"Right, that's all we can do for tonight," said Dad. "We've told them who we are and where to find us, so we'll wait 'til tomorrow night and see if we get an answer."

Mum looked at Emily's beaming face. "Don't get too excited," she said gently. "We may hear nothing more. It might be a lonely old dragon, not the young friend you're hoping for. And it is a long way away. Bedtime now!"

All through the next day, while she foraged for snails and played in the woods with Tom and the little otters, Emily saw again in her mind that thin plume of smoke and wondered who had huffed it. She was too excited to eat much supper, and as soon as the sun set, the whole family flew up to Ben's head. Tom perched on his favourite ear as usual. They all gazed south, and in a few minutes the smoke was seen again, but nearer – much nearer.

"He says he's on his way," said Dad, after he had studied the signals, "but that's all. Nothing about who he is, or whether he's on his own. I'll send a reply." He huffed busily, and Mum explained that he was telling the strange dragon he'd be welcome and sending directions. Two tiny puffs were sent in return.

"I bet that says O.K." said Tom.

Dad laughed. "More or less," he said, "but he won't be here yet, so an early night for us all, I think, and we'll see what sort of dragon turns up tomorrow!"

For more information on the Dragon Tales books, email info@alisonjones.com.